The Boarding-House

by

Charles Dickens

Rise of Douai

Copyright © 2014 Rise of Douai

All rights reserved.

ISBN-13:
978-1502512567

ISBN-10:
1502512564

Introduction

The boarding-house is a short story by Charles Dickens.

Charles John Huffam Dickens (7 February 1812 – 9 June 1870) was an English writer and social critic. He created some of the world's most memorable fictional characters and is generally regarded as the greatest novelist of the Victorian period. During his life, his works enjoyed unprecedented fame, and by the twentieth century his literary genius was broadly acknowledged by critics and scholars. His novels and short stories continue to be widely popular.

Born in Portsmouth, England, Dickens was forced to leave school to work in a factory when his father was thrown into debtors' prison. Although he had little formal education, his early impoverishment drove him to succeed. Over his career he edited a weekly journal for 20 years, wrote 15 novels, five novellas and hundreds of short stories and non-fiction articles, lectured and performed extensively, was an indefatigable letter writer, and campaigned vigorously for children's rights, education, and other social reforms.

Dickens sprang to fame with the 1836 serial publication of The Pickwick Papers. Within a few years he had become an international literary celebrity, famous for his humour, satire, and keen observation of character and society. His novels, most published in monthly or weekly installments, pioneered the serial publication of narrative fiction, which became the dominant Victorian mode for novel publication. The installment format allowed Dickens to evaluate his audience's reaction, and he often modified his plot and character development based on such feedback. For example, when his wife's chiropodist expressed distress at the way Miss Mowcher in David Copperfield seemed to reflect her disabilities, Dickens went on to improve the character with positive features. Fagin in Oliver Twist apparently mirrors the famous fence Ikey Solomon; His caricature of Leigh Hunt in the figure of Mr Skimpole in Bleak House was likewise toned down on advice from some of his friends, as they read episodes. In the same novel, both Lawrence Boythorne and Mooney the beadle are drawn from real life—Boythorne from Walter Savage Landor and Mooney from 'Looney', a beadle at Salisbury Square. His plots were carefully constructed, and Dickens often wove in elements from topical events into his narratives. Masses of the illiterate poor chipped in ha'pennies to have each new monthly episode read to them, opening up and inspiring a new class of readers.

The boarding-house

<u>Chapter the first</u>..............................4
<u>Chapter the second</u>.....................33

Chapter the First

Mrs. Tibbs was, beyond all dispute, the most tidy, fidgety, thrifty little personage that ever inhaled the smoke of London; and the house of Mrs. Tibbs was, decidedly, the neatest in all Great Coram-street. The area and the area-steps, and the street-door and the street-door steps, and the brass handle, and the door-plate, and the knocker, and the fan-light, were all as clean and bright, as indefatigable white-washing, and hearth-stoning, and scrubbing and rubbing, could make them. The wonder was, that the brass door-plate, with the interesting inscription 'MRS. TIBBS,' had never caught fire from constant friction, so perseveringly was it polished. There were meat-safe-looking blinds in the parlour-windows, blue and gold curtains in the drawing-room, and spring-roller blinds, as Mrs. Tibbs was wont in the pride of her heart to boast, 'all the way up.' The bell-lamp in the passage looked as clear as a soap-bubble; you could see yourself in all the tables, and French-polish yourself on any one of the chairs. The banisters were bees-waxed; and the very stair-wires made your eyes wink, they were so glittering.

Mrs. Tibbs was somewhat short of stature, and Mr. Tibbs was by no means a large man. He had, moreover, very short legs, but, by way of indemnification, his face was peculiarly long. He was to his wife what the 0 is in 90—he was of some importance with her—he was nothing without her.

Mrs. Tibbs was always talking. Mr. Tibbs rarely spoke; but, if it were at any time possible to put in a word, when he should have said nothing at all, he had that talent. Mrs. Tibbs detested long stories, and Mr. Tibbs had one, the conclusion of which had never been heard by his most intimate friends. It always began, 'I recollect when I was in the volunteer corps, in eighteen hundred and six,'—but, as he spoke very slowly and softly, and his better half very quickly and loudly, he rarely got beyond the introductory sentence. He was a melancholy specimen of the story-teller. He was the wandering Jew of Joe Millerism.

Mr. Tibbs enjoyed a small independence from the pension-list—about 43l. 15s. 10d. a year. His father, mother, and five interesting scions from the same stock, drew a like sum from the revenue of a grateful country, though for what particular service was never known. But, as this said independence was not quite sufficient to furnish two people with all the luxuries of this life, it had occurred to the busy little spouse of Tibbs, that the best thing she could do with a legacy of 700l., would be to take and furnish a tolerable house— somewhere in that partially-explored tract of country which lies between the British Museum, and a remote village called Somers-town—for the reception of boarders. Great Coram-street was the spot pitched upon. The house had been furnished accordingly; two female servants and a boy engaged; and an advertisement inserted in the morning papers, informing the public that 'Six individuals would meet with all the comforts of a cheerful musical home in a select private family, residing within ten minutes' walk of'—everywhere. Answers out of number were received, with all sorts of initials; all the letters of the alphabet seemed to be seized with a sudden wish to go out boarding and lodging; voluminous was the correspondence between Mrs. Tibbs and the applicants; and most profound was the secrecy observed. 'E.' didn't like this; 'I.' couldn't think of putting up with that; 'I. O. U.' didn't think the terms would suit him; and 'G. R.' had never slept in a French bed. The result, however, was, that three gentlemen became inmates of Mrs. Tibbs's house, on terms which were 'agreeable to all parties.' In went the advertisement again, and a lady with her two daughters, proposed to increase—not their families, but Mrs. Tibbs's.

'Charming woman, that Mrs. Maplesone!' said Mrs. Tibbs, as she and her spouse were sitting by the fire after breakfast; the gentlemen having gone out on their several avocations. 'Charming woman, indeed!' repeated little Mrs. Tibbs, more by way of soliloquy than anything else, for she never thought of consulting her husband. 'And the two daughters are delightful. We must have some fish to-day; they'll join us at dinner for the first time.'

Mr. Tibbs placed the poker at right angles with the fire shovel, and essayed to speak, but recollected he had nothing to say.

'The young ladies,' continued Mrs. T., 'have kindly

volunteered to bring their own piano.'

Tibbs thought of the volunteer story, but did not venture it.

A bright thought struck him -

'It's very likely—' said he.

'Pray don't lean your head against the paper,' interrupted Mrs. Tibbs; 'and don't put your feet on the steel fender; that's worse.'

Tibbs took his head from the paper, and his feet from the fender, and proceeded. 'It's very likely one of the young ladies may set her cap at young Mr. Simpson, and you know a marriage—'

'A what!' shrieked Mrs. Tibbs. Tibbs modestly repeated his former suggestion.

'I beg you won't mention such a thing,' said Mrs. T. 'A marriage, indeed to rob me of my boarders—no, not for the world.'

Tibbs thought in his own mind that the event was by no means unlikely, but, as he never argued with his wife, he put a stop to the dialogue, by observing it was 'time to go to business.' He always went out at ten o'clock in the morning, and returned at five in the afternoon, with an exceedingly dirty face, and smelling mouldy. Nobody knew what he was, or where he went;

but Mrs. Tibbs used to say with an air of great importance, that he was engaged in the City.

The Miss Maplesones and their accomplished parent arrived in the course of the afternoon in a hackney-coach, and accompanied by a most astonishing number of packages. Trunks, bonnet-boxes, muff-boxes and parasols, guitar-cases, and parcels of all imaginable shapes, done up in brown paper, and fastened with pins, filled the passage. Then, there was such a running up and down with the luggage, such scampering for warm water for the ladies to wash in, and such a bustle, and confusion, and heating of servants, and curling-irons, as had never been known in Great Coram-street before. Little Mrs. Tibbs was quite in her element, bustling about, talking incessantly, and distributing towels and soap, like a head nurse in a hospital. The house was not restored to its usual state of quiet repose, until the ladies were safely shut up in their respective bedrooms, engaged in the important occupation of dressing for dinner.

'Are these gals 'andsome?' inquired Mr. Simpson of Mr. Septimus Hicks, another of the boarders, as they were amusing themselves in the drawing-room, before dinner, by lolling on sofas, and contemplating their pumps.

'Don't know,' replied Mr. Septimus Hicks, who was a tallish, white-faced young man, with spectacles, and a black ribbon round his neck instead of a neckerchief— a most interesting person; a poetical walker of the hospitals, and a 'very talented young man.' He was fond of 'lugging' into conversation all sorts of quotations from Don Juan, without fettering himself by the propriety of their application; in which particular he was remarkably independent. The other, Mr. Simpson, was one of those young men, who are in society what walking gentlemen are on the stage, only infinitely worse skilled in his vocation than the most indifferent artist. He was as empty-headed as the great bell of St. Paul's; always dressed according to the caricatures published in the monthly fashion; and spelt Character with a K.

'I saw a devilish number of parcels in the passage when I came home,' simpered Mr. Simpson.

'Materials for the toilet, no doubt,' rejoined the Don Juan reader.

- 'Much linen, lace, and several pair Of stockings, slippers, brushes, combs, complete; With other articles of ladies fair, To keep them beautiful, or leave them neat.'

'Is that from Milton?' inquired Mr. Simpson.

'No—from Byron,' returned Mr. Hicks, with a look of contempt. He was quite sure of his author, because he had never read any other. 'Hush! Here come the gals,' and they both commenced talking in a very loud key.

'Mrs. Maplesone and the Miss Maplesones, Mr. Hicks. Mr. Hicks—Mrs. Maplesone and the Miss Maplesones,' said Mrs. Tibbs, with a very red face, for she had been superintending the cooking operations below stairs, and looked like a wax doll on a sunny day. 'Mr. Simpson, I beg your pardon—Mr. Simpson—Mrs. Maplesone and the Miss Maplesones'—and vice versâ. The gentlemen immediately began to slide about with much politeness, and to look as if they wished their arms had been legs, so little did they know what to do with them. The ladies smiled, curtseyed, and glided into chairs, and dived for dropped pocket-handkerchiefs: the gentlemen leant against two of the curtain-pegs; Mrs. Tibbs went through an admirable bit of serious pantomime with a servant who had come up to ask some question about the fish-sauce; and then the two young ladies looked at each other; and everybody else appeared to discover something very attractive in the pattern of the fender.

'Julia, my love,' said Mrs. Maplesone to her youngest daughter, in a tone loud enough for the remainder of the company to hear—'Julia.'

'Yes, Ma.'

'Don't stoop.'—This was said for the purpose of directing general attention to Miss Julia's figure, which was undeniable. Everybody looked at her, accordingly, and there was another pause.

'We had the most uncivil hackney-coachman to-day, you can imagine,' said Mrs. Maplesone to Mrs. Tibbs, in a confidential tone.

'Dear me!' replied the hostess, with an air of great commiseration. She couldn't say more, for the servant again appeared at the door, and commenced telegraphing most earnestly to her 'Missis.'

'I think hackney-coachmen generally are uncivil,' said Mr. Hicks in his most insinuating tone.

'Positively I think they are,' replied Mrs. Maplesone, as if the idea had never struck her before.

'And cabmen, too,' said Mr. Simpson. This remark was a failure, for no one intimated, by word or sign, the slightest knowledge of the manners and customs of cabmen.

'Robinson, what do you want?' said Mrs. Tibbs to the servant, who, by way of making her presence known to her mistress, had been giving sundry hems and sniffs outside the door during the preceding five minutes.

'Please, ma'am, master wants his clean things,' replied the servant, taken off her guard. The two young men turned their faces to the window, and 'went off' like a couple of bottles of ginger-beer; the ladies put their handkerchiefs to their mouths; and little Mrs. Tibbs bustled out of the room to give Tibbs his clean linen,—and the servant warning.

Mr. Calton, the remaining boarder, shortly afterwards made his appearance, and proved a surprising promoter of the conversation. Mr. Calton was a superannuated beau—an old boy. He used to say of himself that although his features were not regularly handsome, they were striking. They certainly were. It was impossible to look at his face without being reminded of a chubby street-door knocker, half-lion half-monkey; and the comparison might be extended to his whole character and conversation. He had stood still, while everything else had been moving. He never originated a conversation, or started an idea; but if any commonplace topic were broached, or, to pursue the comparison, if anybody lifted him up, he would hammer away with surprising rapidity. He had the tic-douloureux occasionally, and then he might be said to be muffled, because he did not make quite as much noise as at other times, when he would go on prosing, rat-tat-tat the same thing over and over again. He had never been married; but he was still on the look-out for a wife with money. He had a life interest worth about 300l. a year—he was exceedingly vain, and inordinately selfish. He had acquired the reputation of being the very pink of politeness, and he walked round the park, and up Regent-street, every day.

This respectable personage had made up his mind to render himself exceedingly agreeable to Mrs. Maplesone—indeed, the desire of being as amiable as possible extended itself to the whole party; Mrs. Tibbs having considered it an admirable little bit of management to represent to the gentlemen that she had some reason to believe the ladies were fortunes, and to hint to the ladies, that all the gentlemen were 'eligible.' A little flirtation, she thought, might keep her house full, without leading to any other result.

Mrs. Maplesone was an enterprising widow of about fifty: shrewd, scheming, and good-looking. She was amiably anxious on behalf of her daughters; in proof whereof she used to remark, that she would have no objection to marry again, if it would benefit her dear girls—she could have no other motive. The 'dear girls' themselves were not at all insensible to the merits of 'a good establishment.' One of them was twenty-five; the other, three years younger. They had been at different watering-places, for four seasons; they had gambled at libraries, read books in balconies, sold at fancy fairs, danced at assemblies, talked sentiment—in short, they had done all that industrious girls could do—but, as yet, to no purpose.

'What a magnificent dresser Mr. Simpson is!' whispered Matilda Maplesone to her sister Julia.

'Splendid!' returned the youngest. The magnificent individual alluded to wore a maroon-coloured dress-coat, with a velvet collar and cuffs of the same tint—very like that which usually invests the form of the distinguished unknown who condescends to play the 'swell' in the pantomime at 'Richardson's Show.'

'What whiskers!' said Miss Julia.

'Charming!' responded her sister; 'and what hair!' His hair was like a wig, and distinguished by that insinuating wave which graces the shining locks of those chef-d'oeuvres of art surmounting the waxen images in Bartellot's window in Regent-street; his whiskers meeting beneath his chin, seemed strings wherewith to tie it on, ere science had rendered them unnecessary by her patent invisible springs.

'Dinner's on the table, ma'am, if you please,' said the boy, who now appeared for the first time, in a revived black coat of his master's.

'Oh! Mr. Calton, will you lead Mrs. Maplesone?— Thank you.' Mr. Simpson offered his arm to Miss Julia; Mr. Septimus Hicks escorted the lovely Matilda; and the procession proceeded to the dining-room. Mr. Tibbs was introduced, and Mr. Tibbs bobbed up and down to the three ladies like a figure in a Dutch clock, with a powerful spring in the middle of his body, and then dived rapidly into his seat at the bottom of the table, delighted to screen himself behind a soup-tureen, which he could just see over, and that was all. The boarders were seated, a lady and gentleman alternately, like the layers of bread and meat in a plate of sandwiches; and then Mrs. Tibbs directed James to take off the covers. Salmon, lobster-sauce, giblet-soup, and the usual accompaniments were discovered: potatoes like petrifactions, and bits of toasted bread, the shape and size of blank dice.

'Soup for Mrs. Maplesone, my dear,' said the

bustling Mrs. Tibbs. She always called her husband 'my dear' before company. Tibbs, who had been eating his bread, and calculating how long it would be before he should get any fish, helped the soup in a hurry, made a small island on the table-cloth, and put his glass upon it, to hide it from his wife.

'Miss Julia, shall I assist you to some fish?'

'If you please—very little—oh! plenty, thank you' (a bit about the size of a walnut put upon the plate).

'Julia is a very little eater,' said Mrs. Maplesone to Mr. Calton.

The knocker gave a single rap. He was busy eating the fish with his eyes: so he only ejaculated, 'Ah!'

'My dear,' said Mrs. Tibbs to her spouse after every one else had been helped, 'what do you take?' The inquiry was accompanied with a look intimating that he mustn't say fish, because there was not much left. Tibbs thought the frown referred to the island on the table-cloth; he therefore coolly replied, 'Why—I'll take a little—fish, I think.'

'Did you say fish, my dear?' (another frown).

'Yes, dear,' replied the villain, with an expression of acute hunger depicted in his countenance. The tears almost started to Mrs. Tibbs's eyes, as she helped her 'wretch of a husband,' as she inwardly called him, to the last eatable bit of salmon on the dish.

'James, take this to your master, and take away your master's knife.' This was deliberate revenge, as Tibbs never could eat fish without one. He was, however, constrained to chase small particles of salmon round and round his plate with a piece of bread and a fork, the number of successful attempts being about one in seventeen.

'Take away, James,' said Mrs. Tibbs, as Tibbs swallowed the fourth mouthful—and away went the plates like lightning.

'I'll take a bit of bread, James,' said the poor 'master of the house,' more hungry than ever.

'Never mind your master now, James,' said Mrs. Tibbs, 'see about the meat.' This was conveyed in the tone in which ladies usually give admonitions to servants in company, that is to say, a low one; but which, like a stage whisper, from its peculiar emphasis, is most distinctly heard by everybody present.

A pause ensued, before the table was replenished—a sort of parenthesis in which Mr. Simpson, Mr. Calton, and Mr. Hicks, produced respectively a bottle of sauterne, bucellas, and sherry, and took wine with everybody—except Tibbs. No one ever thought of him.

Between the fish and an intimated sirloin, there was

a prolonged interval.

Here was an opportunity for Mr. Hicks. He could not resist the singularly appropriate quotation -

'But beef is rare within these oxless isles; Goats' flesh there is, no doubt, and kid, and mutton, And when a holiday upon them smiles, A joint upon their barbarous spits they put on.'

'Very ungentlemanly behaviour,' thought little Mrs. Tibbs, 'to talk in that way.'

'Ah,' said Mr. Calton, filling his glass. 'Tom Moore is my poet.'

'And mine,' said Mrs. Maplesone.

'And mine,' said Miss Julia.

'And mine,' added Mr. Simpson.

'Look at his compositions,' resumed the knocker.

'To be sure,' said Simpson, with confidence.

'Look at Don Juan,' replied Mr. Septimus Hicks.

'Julia's letter,' suggested Miss Matilda.

'Can anything be grander than the Fire Worshippers?' inquired Miss Julia.

'To be sure,' said Simpson.
'Or Paradise and the Peri,' said the old beau.

'Yes; or Paradise and the Peer,' repeated Simpson, who thought he was getting through it capitally.

'It's all very well,' replied Mr. Septimus Hicks, who, as we have before hinted, never had read anything but Don Juan. 'Where will you find anything finer than the description of the siege, at the commencement of the seventh canto?'

'Talking of a siege,' said Tibbs, with a mouthful of bread—'when I was in the volunteer corps, in eighteen hundred and six, our commanding officer was Sir Charles Rampart; and one day, when we were exercising on the ground on which the London University now stands, he says, says he, Tibbs (calling me from the ranks), Tibbs—'

'Tell your master, James,' interrupted Mrs. Tibbs, in an awfully distinct tone, 'tell your master if he won't carve those fowls, to send them to me.' The discomfited volunteer instantly set to work, and carved the fowls almost as expeditiously as his wife operated on the haunch of mutton. Whether he ever finished the story is not known but, if he did, nobody heard it.

As the ice was now broken, and the new inmates more at home, every member of the company felt more at ease. Tibbs himself most certainly did, because he went to sleep immediately after dinner. Mr. Hicks and the ladies discoursed most eloquently about poetry, and the theatres, and Lord Chesterfield's Letters; and Mr. Calton followed up what everybody said, with continuous double knocks. Mrs. Tibbs highly approved of every observation that fell from Mrs. Maplesone; and as Mr. Simpson sat with a smile upon his face and said 'Yes,' or 'Certainly,' at intervals of about four minutes each, he received full credit for understanding what was going forward. The gentlemen rejoined the ladies in the drawing-room very shortly after they had left the dining-parlour. Mrs. Maplesone and Mr. Calton played cribbage, and the 'young people' amused themselves with music and conversation. The Miss Maplesones sang the most fascinating duets, and accompanied themselves on guitars, ornamented with bits of ethereal blue ribbon. Mr. Simpson put on a pink waistcoat, and said he was in raptures; and Mr. Hicks felt in the seventh heaven of poetry or the seventh canto of Don Juan—it was the same thing to him. Mrs. Tibbs was quite charmed with the newcomers; and Mr. Tibbs spent the evening in his usual way—he went to sleep, and woke up, and went to sleep again, and woke at supper-time.

* * * * *

We are not about to adopt the licence of novel-writers, and to let 'years roll on;' but we will take the liberty of requesting the reader to suppose that six months have elapsed, since the dinner we have described, and that Mrs. Tibbs's boarders have, during that period, sang, and danced, and gone to theatres and exhibitions, together, as ladies and gentlemen, wherever they board, often do. And we will beg them, the period we have mentioned having elapsed, to imagine farther, that Mr. Septimus Hicks received, in his own bedroom (a front attic), at an early hour one morning, a note from Mr. Calton, requesting the favour of seeing him, as soon as convenient to himself, in his (Calton's) dressing-room on the second-floor back.

'Tell Mr. Calton I'll come down directly,' said Mr. Septimus to the boy. 'Stop—is Mr. Calton unwell?' inquired this excited walker of hospitals, as he put on a bed-furniture-looking dressing-gown.

'Not as I knows on, sir,' replied the boy. ' Please, sir, he looked rather rum, as it might be.'

'Ah, that's no proof of his being ill,' returned Hicks, unconsciously. 'Very well: I'll be down directly.' Downstairs ran the boy with the message, and down went the excited Hicks himself, almost as soon as the message was delivered. 'Tap, tap.' 'Come in.'—Door opens, and discovers Mr. Calton sitting in an easy chair. Mutual shakes of the hand exchanged, and Mr. Septimus Hicks motioned to a seat. A short pause. Mr. Hicks coughed, and Mr. Calton took a pinch of snuff. It was one of those interviews where neither party knows what to say. Mr. Septimus Hicks broke silence.

'I received a note—' he said, very tremulously, in a voice like a Punch with a cold.

'Yes,' returned the other, 'you did.'
'Exactly.'

'Yes.'

Now, although this dialogue must have been satisfactory, both gentlemen felt there was something more important to be said; therefore they did as most men in such a situation would have done—they looked at the table with a determined aspect. The conversation had been opened, however, and Mr. Calton had made up his mind to continue it with a regular double knock. He always spoke very pompously.

'Hicks,' said he, 'I have sent for you, in consequence of certain arrangements which are pending in this house, connected with a marriage.'

'With a marriage!' gasped Hicks, compared with whose expression of countenance, Hamlet's, when he sees his father's ghost, is pleasing and composed.

'With a marriage,' returned the knocker. 'I have sent for you to prove the great confidence I can repose in you.'

'And will you betray me?' eagerly inquired Hicks, who in his alarm had even forgotten to quote.

'I betray you! Won't you betray me?'

'Never: no one shall know, to my dying day, that you had a hand in the business,' responded the agitated Hicks, with an inflamed countenance, and his hair standing on end as if he were on the stool of an electrifying machine in full operation.

'People must know that, some time or other—within a year, I imagine,' said Mr. Calton, with an air of great self-complacency. 'We may have a family.'

'We!—That won't affect you, surely?'

'The devil it won't!'

'No! how can it?' said the bewildered Hicks. Calton was too much inwrapped in the contemplation of his happiness to see the equivoque between Hicks and himself; and threw himself back in his chair. 'Oh, Matilda!' sighed the antique beau, in a lack-a-daisical voice, and applying his right hand a little to the left of the fourth button of his waistcoat, counting from the bottom. 'Oh, Matilda!'

'What Matilda?' inquired Hicks, starting up.

'Matilda Maplesone,' responded the other, doing the same.

'I marry her to-morrow morning,' said Hicks.

'It's false,' rejoined his companion: 'I marry her!'

'You marry her?'
'I marry her!'

'You marry Matilda Maplesone?'

'Matilda Maplesone.'

'Miss Maplesone marry you?'

'Miss Maplesone! No; Mrs. Maplesone.'

'Good Heaven!' said Hicks, falling into his chair: 'You marry the mother, and I the daughter!'

'Most extraordinary circumstance!' replied Mr. Calton, 'and rather inconvenient too; for the fact is, that owing to Matilda's wishing to keep her intention secret from her daughters until the ceremony had taken place, she doesn't like applying to any of her friends to give her away. I entertain an objection to making the affair known to my acquaintance just now; and the consequence is, that I sent to you to know whether you'd oblige me by acting as father.'

'I should have been most happy, I assure you,' said Hicks, in a tone of condolence; 'but, you see, I shall be acting as bridegroom. One character is frequently a consequence of the other; but it is not usual to act in both at the same time. There's Simpson—I have no doubt he'll do it for you.'

'I don't like to ask him,' replied Calton, 'he's such a donkey.'

Mr. Septimus Hicks looked up at the ceiling, and down at the floor; at last an idea struck him. 'Let the man of the house, Tibbs, be the father,' he suggested; and then he quoted, as peculiarly applicable to Tibbs and the pair -

'Oh Powers of Heaven! what dark eyes meets she there? "Tis—'tis her father's—fixed upon the pair.'

'The idea has struck me already,' said Mr. Calton: 'but, you see, Matilda, for what reason I know not, is very anxious that Mrs. Tibbs should know nothing about it, till it's all over. It's a natural delicacy, after all, you know.'

'He's the best-natured little man in existence, if you manage him properly,' said Mr. Septimus Hicks. 'Tell him not to mention it to his wife, and assure him she won't mind it, and he'll do it directly. My marriage is to be a secret one, on account of the mother and my father; therefore he must be enjoined to secrecy.'

A small double knock, like a presumptuous single one, was that instant heard at the street-door. It was Tibbs; it could be no one else; for no one else occupied five minutes in rubbing his shoes. He had been out to pay the baker's bill.

'Mr. Tibbs,' called Mr. Calton in a very bland tone, looking over the banisters.

'Sir!' replied he of the dirty face.

'Will you have the kindness to step up-stairs for a moment?'

'Certainly, sir,' said Tibbs, delighted to be taken notice of. The bedroom-door was carefully closed, and Tibbs, having put his hat on the floor (as most timid men do), and been accommodated with a seat, looked as astounded as if he were suddenly summoned before the familiars of the Inquisition.

'A rather unpleasant occurrence, Mr. Tibbs,' said Calton, in a very portentous manner, 'obliges me to consult you, and to beg you will not communicate what I am about to say, to your wife.'

Tibbs acquiesced, wondering in his own mind what the deuce the other could have done, and imagining that at least he must have broken the best decanters.

Mr. Calton resumed; 'I am placed, Mr. Tibbs, in rather an unpleasant situation.'

Tibbs looked at Mr. Septimus Hicks, as if he thought Mr. H.'s being in the immediate vicinity of his fellow-boarder might constitute the unpleasantness of his situation; but as he did not exactly know what to say, he merely ejaculated the monosyllable 'Lor!'

'Now,' continued the knocker, 'let me beg you will exhibit no manifestations of surprise, which may be overheard by the domestics, when I tell you—command your feelings of astonishment—that two inmates of this house intend to be married to-morrow morning.' And he drew back his chair, several feet, to perceive the effect of the unlooked-for announcement.

If Tibbs had rushed from the room, staggered down-stairs, and fainted in the passage—if he had instantaneously jumped out of the window into the mews behind the house, in an agony of surprise—his behaviour would have been much less inexplicable to Mr. Calton than it was, when he put his hands into his inexpressible-pockets, and said with a half-chuckle, 'Just so.'

'You are not surprised, Mr. Tibbs?' inquired Mr. Calton.

'Bless you, no, sir,' returned Tibbs; 'after all, its very natural. When two young people get together, you know—'

'Certainly, certainly,' said Calton, with an indescribable air of self-satisfaction.

'You don't think it's at all an out-of-the-way affair then?' asked Mr. Septimus Hicks, who had watched the countenance of Tibbs in mute astonishment.

'No, sir,' replied Tibbs; 'I was just the same at his age.' He actually smiled when he said this.

'How devilish well I must carry my years!' thought the delighted old beau, knowing he was at least ten years older than Tibbs at that moment.

'Well, then, to come to the point at once,' he continued, 'I have to ask you whether you will object to act as father on the occasion?'

'Certainly not,' replied Tibbs; still without evincing an atom of surprise.

'You will not?'

'Decidedly not,' reiterated Tibbs, still as calm as a pot of porter with the head off.

Mr. Calton seized the hand of the petticoat-governed little man, and vowed eternal friendship from that hour. Hicks, who was all admiration and surprise, did the same.

'Now, confess,' asked Mr. Calton of Tibbs, as he picked up his hat, 'were you not a little surprised?'

'I b'lieve you!' replied that illustrious person, holding up one hand; 'I b'lieve you! When I first heard of it.'

'So sudden,' said Septimus Hicks.

'So strange to ask me, you know,' said Tibbs.

'So odd altogether!' said the superannuated love-maker; and then all three laughed.

'I say,' said Tibbs, shutting the door which he had previously opened, and giving full vent to a hitherto corked-up giggle, 'what bothers me is, what will his father say?'

Mr. Septimus Hicks looked at Mr. Calton.

'Yes; but the best of it is,' said the latter, giggling in his turn, 'I haven't got a father—he! he! he!'

'You haven't got a father. No; but he has,' said Tibbs.

'Who has?' inquired Septimus Hicks.

'Why, him.'

'Him, who? Do you know my secret? Do you mean me?'

'You! No; you know who I mean,' returned Tibbs with a knowing wink.

'For Heaven's sake, whom do you mean?' inquired Mr. Calton, who, like Septimus Hicks, was all but out of his senses at the strange confusion.

'Why Mr. Simpson, of course,' replied Tibbs; 'who else could I mean?'

'I see it all,' said the Byron-quoter; 'Simpson marries Julia Maplesone to-morrow morning!'

'Undoubtedly,' replied Tibbs, thoroughly satisfied, 'of course he does.'

It would require the pencil of Hogarth to illustrate—our feeble pen is inadequate to describe—the expression which the countenances of Mr. Calton and Mr. Septimus Hicks respectively assumed, at this unexpected announcement. Equally impossible is it to describe, although perhaps it is easier for our lady readers to imagine, what arts the three ladies could have used, so completely to entangle their separate partners. Whatever they were, however, they were successful. The mother was perfectly aware of the intended marriage of both daughters; and the young ladies were equally acquainted with the intention of their estimable parent. They agreed, however, that it would have a much better appearance if each feigned ignorance of the other's engagement; and it was equally desirable that all the marriages should take place on the same day, to prevent the discovery of one clandestine alliance, operating prejudicially on the others. Hence, the mystification of Mr. Calton and Mr. Septimus Hicks, and the pre-engagement of the unwary Tibbs.

On the following morning, Mr. Septimus Hicks was united to Miss Matilda Maplesone. Mr. Simpson also entered into a 'holy alliance' with Miss Julia; Tibbs acting as father, 'his first appearance in that character.' Mr. Calton, not being quite so eager as the two young men, was rather struck by the double discovery; and as he had found some difficulty in getting any one to give the lady away, it occurred to him that the best mode of obviating the inconvenience would be not to take her at all. The lady, however, 'appealed,' as her counsel said on the trial of the cause, Maplesone v. Calton, for a breach of promise, 'with a broken heart, to the outraged laws of her country.' She recovered damages to the amount of 1,000l. which the unfortunate knocker was compelled to pay. Mr. Septimus Hicks having walked the hospitals, took it into his head to walk off altogether. His injured wife is at present residing with her mother at Boulogne. Mr. Simpson, having the misfortune to lose his wife six weeks after marriage (by her eloping with an officer during his temporary sojourn in the Fleet Prison, in consequence of his inability to discharge her little mantua-maker's bill), and being disinherited by his father, who died soon afterwards, was fortunate enough to obtain a permanent engagement at a fashionable haircutter's; hairdressing being a science to which he had frequently directed his attention. In this situation he had necessarily many opportunities of making himself acquainted with the habits, and style of thinking, of the exclusive portion of the nobility of this kingdom. To this fortunate circumstance are we indebted for the production of those brilliant efforts of genius, his fashionable novels, which so long as good taste, unsullied by exaggeration, cant, and quackery, continues to exist, cannot fail to instruct and amuse the thinking portion of the community.

It only remains to add, that this complication of disorders completely deprived poor Mrs. Tibbs of all her inmates, except the one whom she could have best spared—her husband. That wretched little man returned home, on the day of the wedding, in a state of partial intoxication; and, under the influence of wine, excitement, and despair, actually dared to brave the anger of his wife. Since that ill-fated hour he has constantly taken his meals in the kitchen, to which apartment, it is understood, his witticisms will be in future confined: a turn-up bedstead having been conveyed there by Mrs. Tibbs's order for his exclusive accommodation. It is possible that he will be enabled to finish, in that seclusion, his story of the volunteers.

The advertisement has again appeared in the morning papers. Results must be reserved for another chapter.

Chapter the second

'Well!' said little Mrs. Tibbs to herself, as she sat in the front parlour of the Coram-street mansion one morning, mending a piece of stair-carpet off the first Landings;—'Things have not turned out so badly, either, and if I only get a favourable answer to the advertisement, we shall be full again.'

Mrs. Tibbs resumed her occupation of making worsted lattice-work in the carpet, anxiously listening to the twopenny postman, who was hammering his way down the street, at the rate of a penny a knock. The house was as quiet as possible. There was only one low sound to be heard—it was the unhappy Tibbs cleaning the gentlemen's boots in the back kitchen, and accompanying himself with a buzzing noise, in wretched mockery of humming a tune.

The postman drew near the house. He paused—so did Mrs. Tibbs. A knock—a bustle—a letter—post-paid.

'T. I. presents compt. to I. T. and T. I. begs To say that i see the advertisement And she will Do Herself the pleasure of calling On you at 12 o'clock to-morrow morning.

'T. I. as To apologise to I. T. for the shortness Of

the notice But i hope it will not unconvenience you.

'I remain yours Truly

'Wednesday evening.'

Little Mrs. Tibbs perused the document, over and over again; and the more she read it, the more was she confused by the mixture of the first and third person; the substitution of the 'i' for the 'T. I.;' and the transition from the 'I. T.' to the 'You.' The writing looked like a skein of thread in a tangle, and the note was ingeniously folded into a perfect square, with the direction squeezed up into the right-hand corner, as if it were ashamed of itself. The back of the epistle was pleasingly ornamented with a large red wafer, which, with the addition of divers ink-stains, bore a marvellous resemblance to a black beetle trodden upon. One thing, however, was perfectly clear to the perplexed Mrs. Tibbs. Somebody was to call at twelve. The drawing-room was forthwith dusted for the third time that morning; three or four chairs were pulled out of their places, and a corresponding number of books carefully upset, in order that there might be a due absence of formality. Down went the piece of stair-carpet before noticed, and up ran Mrs. Tibbs 'to make herself tidy.'

The clock of New Saint Pancras Church struck twelve, and the Foundling, with laudable politeness, did the same ten minutes afterwards, Saint something else struck the quarter, and then there arrived a single lady with a double knock, in a pelisse the colour of the interior of a damson pie; a bonnet of the same, with a regular conservatory of artificial flowers; a white veil, and a green parasol, with a cobweb border.

The visitor (who was very fat and red-faced) was shown into the drawing-room; Mrs. Tibbs presented herself, and the negotiation commenced.

'I called in consequence of an advertisement,' said the stranger, in a voice as if she had been playing a set of Pan's pipes for a fortnight without leaving off.

'Yes!' said Mrs. Tibbs, rubbing her hands very slowly, and looking the applicant full in the face—two things she always did on such occasions.

'Money isn't no object whatever to me,' said the lady, 'so much as living in a state of retirement and obtrusion.'

Mrs. Tibbs, as a matter of course, acquiesced in such an exceedingly natural desire.

'I am constantly attended by a medical man,' resumed the pelisse wearer; 'I have been a shocking unitarian for some time—I, indeed, have had very little peace since the death of Mr. Bloss.'

Mrs. Tibbs looked at the relict of the departed Bloss, and thought he must have had very little peace in his time. Of course she could not say so; so she looked very sympathising.

'I shall be a good deal of trouble to you,' said Mrs. Bloss; 'but, for that trouble I am willing to pay. I am going through a course of treatment which renders attention necessary. I have one mutton-chop in bed at half-past eight, and another at ten, every morning.'

Mrs. Tibbs, as in duty bound, expressed the pity she felt for anybody placed in such a distressing situation; and the carnivorous Mrs. Bloss proceeded to arrange the various preliminaries with wonderful despatch. 'Now mind,' said that lady, after terms were arranged; 'I am to have the second-floor front, for my bedroom?'

'Yes, ma'am.'

'And you'll find room for my little servant Agnes?'

'Oh! certainly.'

'And I can have one of the cellars in the area for my bottled porter.'

'With the greatest pleasure;—James shall get it ready for you by Saturday.'

'And I'll join the company at the breakfast-table on Sunday morning,' said Mrs. Bloss. 'I shall get up on purpose.'

'Very well,' returned Mrs. Tibbs, in her most amiable tone; for satisfactory references had 'been given and required,' and it was quite certain that the new-comer had plenty of money. 'It's rather singular,' continued Mrs. Tibbs, with what was meant for a most bewitching smile, 'that we have a gentleman now with us, who is in a very delicate state of health—a Mr. Gobler.—His apartment is the back drawing-room.'

'The next room?' inquired Mrs. Bloss.

'The next room,' repeated the hostess.

'How very promiscuous!' ejaculated the widow.

'He hardly ever gets up,' said Mrs. Tibbs in a whisper.

'Lor!' cried Mrs. Bloss, in an equally low tone.

'And when he is up,' said Mrs. Tibbs, 'we never can persuade him to go to bed again.'

'Dear me!' said the astonished Mrs. Bloss, drawing her chair nearer Mrs. Tibbs. 'What is his complaint?'

'Why, the fact is,' replied Mrs. Tibbs, with a most communicative air, 'he has no stomach whatever.'

'No what?' inquired Mrs. Bloss, with a look of the most indescribable alarm.

'No stomach,' repeated Mrs. Tibbs, with a shake of the head.

'Lord bless us! what an extraordinary case!' gasped Mrs. Bloss, as if she understood the communication in its literal sense, and was astonished at a gentleman without a stomach finding it necessary to board anywhere.

'When I say he has no stomach,' explained the chatty little Mrs. Tibbs, 'I mean that his digestion is so much impaired, and his interior so deranged, that his stomach is not of the least use to him;—in fact, it's an inconvenience.'

'Never heard such a case in my life!' exclaimed Mrs. Bloss. 'Why, he's worse than I am.'

'Oh, yes!' replied Mrs. Tibbs;—'certainly.' She said this with great confidence, for the damson pelisse suggested that Mrs. Bloss, at all events, was not suffering under Mr. Gobler's complaint.

'You have quite incited my curiosity,' said Mrs. Bloss, as she rose to depart. 'How I long to see him!'

'He generally comes down, once a week,' replied Mrs. Tibbs; 'I dare say you'll see him on Sunday.' With this consolatory promise Mrs. Bloss was obliged to be contented. She accordingly walked slowly down the stairs, detailing her complaints all the way; and Mrs. Tibbs followed her, uttering an exclamation of compassion at every step. James (who looked very gritty, for he was cleaning the knives) fell up the kitchen-stairs, and opened the street-door; and, after mutual farewells, Mrs. Bloss slowly departed, down the shady side of the street.

It is almost superfluous to say, that the lady whom we have just shown out at the street-door (and whom the two female servants are now inspecting from the second-floor windows) was exceedingly vulgar, ignorant, and selfish. Her deceased better-half had been an eminent cork-cutter, in which capacity he had amassed a decent fortune. He had no relative but his nephew, and no friend but his cook. The former had the insolence one morning to ask for the loan of fifteen pounds; and, by way of retaliation, he married the latter next day; he made a will immediately afterwards, containing a burst of honest indignation against his nephew (who supported himself and two sisters on 100l. a year), and a bequest of his whole property to his wife. He felt ill after breakfast, and died after dinner. There is a mantelpiece-looking tablet in a civic parish church, setting forth his virtues, and deploring his loss. He never dishonoured a bill, or gave away a halfpenny.

The relict and sole executrix of this noble-minded man was an odd mixture of shrewdness and simplicity, liberality and meanness. Bred up as she had been, she knew no mode of living so agreeable as a boarding-house: and having nothing to do, and nothing to wish for, she naturally imagined she must be ill—an impression which was most assiduously promoted by her medical attendant, Dr. Wosky, and her handmaid Agnes: both of whom, doubtless for good reasons, encouraged all her extravagant notions.

Since the catastrophe recorded in the last chapter, Mrs. Tibbs had been very shy of young-lady boarders. Her present inmates were all lords of the creation, and she availed herself of the opportunity of their assemblage at the dinner-table, to announce the expected arrival of Mrs. Bloss. The gentlemen received the communication with stoical indifference, and Mrs. Tibbs devoted all her energies to prepare for the reception of the valetudinarian. The second-floor front was scrubbed, and washed, and flannelled, till the wet went through to the drawing-room ceiling. Clean white counterpanes, and curtains, and napkins, water-bottles as clear as crystal, blue jugs, and mahogany furniture, added to the splendour, and increased the comfort, of the apartment. The warming-pan was in constant requisition, and a fire lighted in the room every day. The chattels of Mrs. Bloss were forwarded by instalments. First, there came a large hamper of Guinness's stout, and an umbrella; then, a train of trunks; then, a pair of clogs and a bandbox; then, an easy chair with an air-cushion; then, a variety of suspicious-looking packages; and—'though last not least'—Mrs. Bloss and Agnes: the latter in a cherry-coloured merino dress, open-work stockings, and shoes with sandals: like a disguised Columbine.

The installation of the Duke of Wellington, as

Chancellor of the University of Oxford, was nothing, in point of bustle and turmoil, to the installation of Mrs. Bloss in her new quarters. True, there was no bright doctor of civil law to deliver a classical address on the occasion; but there were several other old women present, who spoke quite as much to the purpose, and understood themselves equally well. The chop-eater was so fatigued with the process of removal that she declined leaving her room until the following morning; so a mutton-chop, pickle, a pill, a pint bottle of stout, and other medicines, were carried up-stairs for her consumption.

'Why, what do you think, ma'am?' inquired the inquisitive Agnes of her mistress, after they had been in the house some three hours; 'what do you think, ma'am? the lady of the house is married.'

'Married!' said Mrs. Bloss, taking the pill and a draught of Guinness—'married! Unpossible!'

'She is indeed, ma'am,' returned the Columbine; 'and her husband, ma'am, lives—he—he—he—lives in the kitchen, ma'am.'

'In the kitchen!'

'Yes, ma'am: and he—he—he—the housemaid says, he never goes into the parlour except on Sundays; and that Ms. Tibbs makes him clean the gentlemen's boots; and that he cleans the windows, too, sometimes; and that one morning early, when he was in the front balcony cleaning the drawing-room windows, he called out to a gentleman on the opposite side of the way, who used to live here—"Ah! Mr. Calton, sir, how are you?"' Here the attendant laughed till Mrs. Bloss was in serious apprehension of her chuckling herself into a fit.

'Well, I never!' said Mrs. Bloss.

'Yes. And please, ma'am, the servants gives him gin-and-water sometimes; and then he cries, and says he hates his wife and the boarders, and wants to tickle them.'

'Tickle the boarders!' exclaimed Mrs. Bloss, seriously alarmed.

'No, ma'am, not the boarders, the servants.'

'Oh, is that all!' said Mrs. Bloss, quite satisfied.

'He wanted to kiss me as I came up the kitchen-stairs, just now,' said Agnes, indignantly; 'but I gave it him—a little wretch!'

This intelligence was but too true. A long course of snubbing and neglect; his days spent in the kitchen, and his nights in the turn-up bedstead, had completely broken the little spirit that the unfortunate volunteer had ever possessed. He had no one to whom he could detail his injuries but the servants, and they were almost of necessity his chosen confidants. It is no less strange than true, however, that the little weaknesses which he had incurred, most probably during his military career, seemed to increase as his comforts diminished. He was actually a sort of journeyman Giovanni of the basement story.

The next morning, being Sunday, breakfast was laid in the front parlour at ten o'clock. Nine was the usual time, but the family always breakfasted an hour later on sabbath. Tibbs enrobed himself in his Sunday costume—a black coat, and exceedingly short, thin trousers; with a very large white waistcoat, white stockings and cravat, and Blucher boots—and mounted to the parlour aforesaid. Nobody had come down, and he amused himself by drinking the contents of the milkpot with a teaspoon.

A pair of slippers were heard descending the stairs. Tibbs flew to a chair; and a stern-looking man, of about fifty, with very little hair on his head, and a Sunday paper in his hand, entered the room.

'Good morning, Mr. Evenson,' said Tibbs, very humbly, with something between a nod and a bow.

'How do you do, Mr. Tibbs?' replied he of the slippers, as he sat himself down, and began to read his paper without saying another word.

'Is Mr. Wisbottle in town to-day, do you know, sir?' inquired Tibbs, just for the sake of saying something.

'I should think he was,' replied the stern gentleman. 'He was whistling "The Light Guitar," in the next room to mine, at five o'clock this morning.'

'He's very fond of whistling,' said Tibbs, with a slight smirk.

'Yes—I ain't,' was the laconic reply.

Mr. John Evenson was in the receipt of an independent income, arising chiefly from various houses he owned in the different suburbs. He was very morose and discontented. He was a thorough radical, and used to attend a great variety of public meetings, for the express purpose of finding fault with everything that was proposed. Mr. Wisbottle, on the other hand, was a high Tory. He was a clerk in the Woods and Forests Office, which he considered rather an aristocratic employment; he knew the peerage by heart, and, could tell you, off-hand, where any illustrious personage lived. He had a good set of teeth, and a capital tailor. Mr. Evenson looked on all these qualifications with profound contempt; and the consequence was that the two were always disputing, much to the edification of the rest of the house. It should be added, that, in addition to his partiality for whistling, Mr. Wisbottle had a great idea of his singing powers. There were two other boarders, besides the gentleman in the back drawing-room—Mr. Alfred Tomkins and Mr. Frederick O'Bleary. Mr. Tomkins was a clerk in a wine-house; he was a connoisseur in paintings, and had a wonderful eye for the picturesque.

Mr. O'Bleary was an Irishman, recently imported; he was in a perfectly wild state; and had come over to England to be an apothecary, a clerk in a government office, an actor, a reporter, or anything else that turned up—he was not particular. He was on familiar terms with two small Irish members, and got franks for everybody in the house. He felt convinced that his intrinsic merits must procure him a high destiny. He wore shepherd's-plaid inexpressibles, and used to look under all the ladies' bonnets as he walked along the streets. His manners and appearance reminded one of Orson.

'Here comes Mr. Wisbottle,' said Tibbs; and Mr. Wisbottle forthwith appeared in blue slippers, and a shawl dressing-gown, whistling 'Di piacer.'

'Good morning, sir,' said Tibbs again. It was almost the only thing he ever said to anybody

'How are you, Tibbs?' condescendingly replied the amateur; and he walked to the window, and whistled louder than ever.

'Pretty air, that!' said Evenson, with a snarl, and without taking his eyes off the paper.

'Glad you like it,' replied Wisbottle, highly gratified.

'Don't you think it would sound better, if you whistled it a little louder?' inquired the mastiff.

'No; I don't think it would,' rejoined the unconscious Wisbottle.

'I'll tell you what, Wisbottle,' said Evenson, who had been bottling up his anger for some hours—'the next time you feel disposed to whistle "The Light Guitar" at five o'clock in the morning, I'll trouble you to whistle it with your head out o' window. If you don't, I'll learn the triangle—I will, by—'

The entrance of Mrs. Tibbs (with the keys in a little basket) interrupted the threat, and prevented its conclusion.

Mrs. Tibbs apologised for being down rather late; the bell was rung; James brought up the urn, and received an unlimited order for dry toast and bacon. Tibbs sat down at the bottom of the table, and began eating water-cresses like a Nebuchadnezzar. Mr. O'Bleary appeared, and Mr. Alfred Tomkins. The compliments of the morning were exchanged, and the tea was made.

'God bless me!' exclaimed Tomkins, who had been looking out at the window. 'Here—Wisbottle—pray come here—make haste.'

Mr. Wisbottle started from the table, and every one looked up.

'Do you see,' said the connoisseur, placing Wisbottle in the right position—'a little more this way:

there—do you see how splendidly the light falls upon the left side of that broken chimney-pot at No. 48?'

'Dear me! I see,' replied Wisbottle, in a tone of admiration.

'I never saw an object stand out so beautifully against the clear sky in my life,' ejaculated Alfred. Everybody (except John Evenson) echoed the sentiment; for Mr. Tomkins had a great character for finding out beauties which no one else could discover—he certainly deserved it.

'I have frequently observed a chimney-pot in College-green, Dublin, which has a much better effect,' said the patriotic O'Bleary, who never allowed Ireland to be outdone on any point.

The assertion was received with obvious incredulity, for Mr. Tomkins declared that no other chimney-pot in the United Kingdom, broken or unbroken, could be so beautiful as the one at No. 48.

The room-door was suddenly thrown open, and Agnes appeared, leading in Mrs. Bloss, who was dressed in a geranium-coloured muslin gown, and displayed a gold watch of huge dimensions; a chain to match; and a splendid assortment of rings, with enormous stones. A general rush was made for a chair, and a regular introduction took place. Mr. John Evenson made a slight inclination of the head; Mr. Frederick O'Bleary, Mr. Alfred Tomkins, and Mr.

Wisbottle, bowed like the mandarins in a grocer's shop; Tibbs rubbed hands, and went round in circles. He was observed to close one eye, and to assume a clock-work sort of expression with the other; this has been considered as a wink, and it has been reported that Agnes was its object. We repel the calumny, and challenge contradiction.

Mrs. Tibbs inquired after Mrs. Bloss's health in a low tone. Mrs. Bloss, with a supreme contempt for the memory of Lindley Murray, answered the various questions in a most satisfactory manner; and a pause ensued, during which the eatables disappeared with awful rapidity.

'You must have been very much pleased with the appearance of the ladies going to the Drawing-room the other day, Mr. O'Bleary?' said Mrs. Tibbs, hoping to start a topic.

'Yes,' replied Orson, with a mouthful of toast.

'Never saw anything like it before, I suppose?' suggested Wisbottle.

'No—except the Lord Lieutenant's levees,' replied O'Bleary.

'Are they at all equal to our drawing-rooms?'

'Oh, infinitely superior!'

'Gad! I don't know,' said the aristocratic Wisbottle, 'the Dowager Marchioness of Publiccash was most magnificently dressed, and so was the Baron Slappenbachenhausen.'

'What was he presented on?' inquired Evenson.

'On his arrival in England.'

'I thought so,' growled the radical; 'you never hear of these fellows being presented on their going away again. They know better than that.'

'Unless somebody pervades them with an apintment,' said Mrs. Bloss, joining in the conversation in a faint voice.

'Well,' said Wisbottle, evading the point, 'it's a splendid sight.'

'And did it never occur to you,' inquired the radical, who never would be quiet; 'did it never occur to you, that you pay for these precious ornaments of society?'

'It certainly has occurred to me,' said Wisbottle, who thought this answer was a poser; 'it has occurred to me, and I am willing to pay for them.'

'Well, and it has occurred to me too,' replied John Evenson, 'and I ain't willing to pay for 'em. Then why should I?—I say, why should I?' continued the politician, laying down the paper, and knocking his knuckles on the table. 'There are two great principles—demand—'

'A cup of tea if you please, dear,' interrupted Tibbs.

'And supply—'

'May I trouble you to hand this tea to Mr. Tibbs?' said Mrs. Tibbs, interrupting the argument, and unconsciously illustrating it.

The thread of the orator's discourse was broken. He drank his tea and resumed the paper.

'If it's very fine,' said Mr. Alfred Tomkins, addressing the company in general, 'I shall ride down to Richmond to-day, and come back by the steamer. There are some splendid effects of light and shade on the Thames; the contrast between the blueness of the sky and the yellow water is frequently exceedingly beautiful.' Mr. Wisbottle hummed, 'Flow on, thou shining river.'

'We have some splendid steam-vessels in Ireland,' said O'Bleary.

'Certainly,' said Mrs. Bloss, delighted to find a subject broached in which she could take part.

'The accommodations are extraordinary,' said O'Bleary.

'Extraordinary indeed,' returned Mrs. Bloss. 'When Mr. Bloss was alive, he was promiscuously obligated to go to Ireland on business. I went with him, and raly the manner in which the ladies and gentlemen were accommodated with berths, is not creditable.'

Tibbs, who had been listening to the dialogue, looked aghast, and evinced a strong inclination to ask a question, but was checked by a look from his wife. Mr. Wisbottle laughed, and said Tomkins had made a pun; and Tomkins laughed too, and said he had not.

The remainder of the meal passed off as breakfasts usually do. Conversation flagged, and people played with their teaspoons. The gentlemen looked out at the window; walked about the room; and, when they got near the door, dropped off one by one. Tibbs retired to the back parlour by his wife's orders, to check the green-grocer's weekly account; and ultimately Mrs. Tibbs and Mrs. Bloss were left alone together.

'Oh dear!' said the latter, 'I feel alarmingly faint; it's very singular.' (It certainly was, for she had eaten four pounds of solids that morning.) 'By-the-bye,' said Mrs. Bloss, 'I have not seen Mr. What's-his-name yet.'

'Mr. Gobler?' suggested Mrs. Tibbs.

'Yes.'

'Oh!' said Mrs. Tibbs, 'he is a most mysterious person. He has his meals regularly sent up-stairs, and sometimes don't leave his room for weeks together.'

'I haven't seen or heard nothing of him,' repeated Mrs. Bloss.

'I dare say you'll hear him to-night,' replied Mrs. Tibbs; 'he generally groans a good deal on Sunday evenings.'

'I never felt such an interest in any one in my life,' ejaculated Mrs. Bloss. A little double-knock interrupted the conversation; Dr. Wosky was announced, and duly shown in. He was a little man with a red face—dressed of course in black, with a stiff white neckerchief. He had a very good practice, and plenty of money, which he had amassed by invariably humouring the worst fancies of all the females of all the families he had ever been introduced into. Mrs. Tibbs offered to retire, but was entreated to stay.

'Well, my dear ma'am, and how are we?' inquired Wosky, in a soothing tone.

'Very ill, doctor—very ill,' said Mrs. Bloss, in a whisper

'Ah! we must take care of ourselves;—we must, indeed,' said the obsequious Wosky, as he felt the pulse of his interesting patient.

'How is our appetite?'

Mrs. Bloss shook her head.

'Our friend requires great care,' said Wosky, appealing to Mrs. Tibbs, who of course assented. 'I hope, however, with the blessing of Providence, that we shall be enabled to make her quite stout again.' Mrs. Tibbs wondered in her own mind what the patient would be when she was made quite stout.

'We must take stimulants,' said the cunning Wosky—'plenty of nourishment, and, above all, we must keep our nerves quiet; we positively must not give way to our sensibilities. We must take all we can get,' concluded the doctor, as he pocketed his fee, 'and we must keep quiet.'

'Dear man!' exclaimed Mrs. Bloss, as the doctor stepped into the carriage.

'Charming creature indeed—quite a lady's man!' said Mrs. Tibbs, and Dr. Wosky rattled away to make fresh gulls of delicate females, and pocket fresh fees.

As we had occasion, in a former paper, to describe a dinner at Mrs. Tibbs's; and as one meal went off very like another on all ordinary occasions; we will not fatigue our readers by entering into any other detailed account of the domestic economy of the establishment. We will therefore proceed to events, merely premising that the mysterious tenant of the back drawing-room was a lazy, selfish hypochondriac; always complaining and never ill. As his character in many respects closely assimilated to that of Mrs. Bloss, a very warm friendship soon sprung up between them. He was tall, thin, and pale; he always fancied he had a severe pain somewhere or other, and his face invariably wore a pinched, screwed-up expression; he looked, indeed, like a man who had got his feet in a tub of exceedingly hot water, against his will.

For two or three months after Mrs. Bloss's first appearance in Coram-street, John Evenson was observed to become, every day, more sarcastic and more ill-natured; and there was a degree of additional importance in his manner, which clearly showed that he fancied he had discovered something, which he only wanted a proper opportunity of divulging. He found it at last.

One evening, the different inmates of the house were assembled in the drawing-room engaged in their ordinary occupations. Mr. Gobler and Mrs. Bloss were sitting at a small card-table near the centre window, playing cribbage; Mr. Wisbottle was describing semicircles on the music-stool, turning over the leaves of a book on the piano, and humming most melodiously; Alfred Tomkins was sitting at the round table, with his elbows duly squared, making a pencil sketch of a head considerably larger than his own; O'Bleary was reading Horace, and trying to look as if he understood it; and John Evenson had drawn his chair close to Mrs. Tibbs's work-table, and was talking to her very earnestly in a low tone.

'I can assure you, Mrs. Tibbs,' said the radical, laying his forefinger on the muslin she was at work on; 'I can assure you, Mrs. Tibbs, that nothing but the interest I take in your welfare would induce me to make this communication. I repeat, I fear Wisbottle is endeavouring to gain the affections of that young woman, Agnes, and that he is in the habit of meeting her in the store-room on the first floor, over the leads. From my bedroom I distinctly heard voices there, last night. I opened my door immediately, and crept very softly on to the landing; there I saw Mr. Tibbs, who, it seems, had been disturbed also.—Bless me, Mrs. Tibbs, you change colour!'

'No, no—it's nothing,' returned Mrs. T. in a hurried manner; 'it's only the heat of the room.'

'A flush!' ejaculated Mrs. Bloss from the card-table; 'that's good for four.'

'If I thought it was Mr. Wisbottle,' said Mrs. Tibbs, after a pause, 'he should leave this house instantly.'

'Go!' said Mrs. Bloss again.

'And if I thought,' continued the hostess with a most threatening air, 'if I thought he was assisted by Mr. Tibbs—'

'One for his nob!' said Gobler.

'Oh,' said Evenson, in a most soothing tone—he

liked to make mischief—'I should hope Mr. Tibbs was not in any way implicated. He always appeared to me very harmless.'

'I have generally found him so,' sobbed poor little Mrs. Tibbs; crying like a watering-pot.

'Hush! hush! pray—Mrs. Tibbs—consider—we shall be observed—pray, don't!' said John Evenson, fearing his whole plan would be interrupted. 'We will set the matter at rest with the utmost care, and I shall be most happy to assist you in doing so.' Mrs. Tibbs murmured her thanks.

'When you think every one has retired to rest tonight,' said Evenson very pompously, 'if you'll meet me without a light, just outside my bedroom door, by the staircase window, I think we can ascertain who the parties really are, and you will afterwards be enabled to proceed as you think proper.'

Mrs. Tibbs was easily persuaded; her curiosity was excited, her jealousy was roused, and the arrangement was forthwith made. She resumed her work, and John Evenson walked up and down the room with his hands in his pockets, looking as if nothing had happened. The game of cribbage was over, and conversation began again.

'Well, Mr. O'Bleary,' said the humming-top, turning round on his pivot, and facing the company, 'what did you think of Vauxhall the other night?'

'Oh, it's very fair,' replied Orson, who had been enthusiastically delighted with the whole exhibition.

'Never saw anything like that Captain Ross's set-out—eh?'

'No,' returned the patriot, with his usual reservation—'except in Dublin.'

'I saw the Count de Canky and Captain Fitzthompson in the Gardens,' said Wisbottle; 'they appeared much delighted.'

'Then it must be beautiful,' snarled Evenson.

'I think the white bears is partickerlerly well done,' suggested Mrs. Bloss. 'In their shaggy white coats, they look just like Polar bears—don't you think they do, Mr. Evenson?'

'I think they look a great deal more like omnibus cads on all fours,' replied the discontented one.

'Upon the whole, I should have liked our evening very well,' gasped Gobler; 'only I caught a desperate cold which increased my pain dreadfully! I was obliged to have several shower-baths, before I could leave my room.'

'Capital things those shower-baths!' ejaculated Wisbottle.

'Excellent!' said Tomkins.

'Delightful!' chimed in O'Bleary. (He had once seen one, outside a tinman's.)

'Disgusting machines!' rejoined Evenson, who extended his dislike to almost every created object, masculine, feminine, or neuter.

'Disgusting, Mr. Evenson!' said Gobler, in a tone of strong indignation.—'Disgusting! Look at their utility—consider how many lives they have saved by promoting perspiration.'

'Promoting perspiration, indeed,' growled John Evenson, stopping short in his walk across the large squares in the pattern of the carpet—'I was ass enough to be persuaded some time ago to have one in my bedroom. 'Gad, I was in it once, and it effectually cured me, for the mere sight of it threw me into a profuse perspiration for six months afterwards.'

A titter followed this announcement, and before it had subsided James brought up 'the tray,' containing the remains of a leg of lamb which had made its début at dinner; bread; cheese; an atom of butter in a forest of parsley; one pickled walnut and the third of another; and so forth. The boy disappeared, and returned again with another tray, containing glasses and jugs of hot and cold water. The gentlemen brought in their spirit-bottles; the housemaid placed divers plated bedroom candlesticks under the card-table; and the servants retired for the night.

Chairs were drawn round the table, and the conversation proceeded in the customary manner. John Evenson, who never ate supper, lolled on the sofa, and amused himself by contradicting everybody. O'Bleary ate as much as he could conveniently carry, and Mrs. Tibbs felt a due degree of indignation thereat; Mr. Gobler and Mrs. Bloss conversed most affectionately on the subject of pill-taking, and other innocent amusements; and Tomkins and Wisbottle 'got into an argument;' that is to say, they both talked very loudly and vehemently, each flattering himself that he had got some advantage about something, and neither of them having more than a very indistinct idea of what they were talking about. An hour or two passed away; and the boarders and the plated candlesticks retired in pairs to their respective bedrooms. John Evenson pulled off his boots, locked his door, and determined to sit up until Mr. Gobler had retired. He always sat in the drawing-room an hour after everybody else had left it, taking medicine, and groaning.

Great Coram-street was hushed into a state of profound repose: it was nearly two o'clock. A hackney-coach now and then rumbled slowly by; and occasionally some stray lawyer's clerk, on his way home to Somers-town, struck his iron heel on the top of the coal-cellar with a noise resembling the click of a smoke-Jack. A low, monotonous, gushing sound was heard, which added considerably to the romantic dreariness of the scene. It was the water 'coming in' at number eleven.

'He must be asleep by this time,' said John Evenson to himself, after waiting with exemplary patience for nearly an hour after Mr. Gobler had left the drawing-room. He listened for a few moments; the house was perfectly quiet; he extinguished his rushlight, and opened his bedroom door. The staircase was so dark that it was impossible to see anything.

'S-s-s!' whispered the mischief-maker, making a noise like the first indication a catherine-wheel gives of the probability of its going off.

'Hush!' whispered somebody else.

'Is that you, Mrs. Tibbs?'

'Yes, sir.'

'Where?'

'Here;' and the misty outline of Mrs. Tibbs appeared at the staircase window, like the ghost of Queen Anne in the tent scene in Richard.

'This way, Mrs. Tibbs,' whispered the delighted busybody: 'give me your hand—there! Whoever these people are, they are in the store-room now, for I have been looking down from my window, and I could see that they accidentally upset their candlestick, and are now in darkness. You have no shoes on, have you?'

'No,' said little Mrs. Tibbs, who could hardly speak for trembling.

'Well; I have taken my boots off, so we can go down, close to the store-room door, and listen over the banisters;' and down-stairs they both crept accordingly, every board creaking like a patent mangle on a Saturday afternoon.

'It's Wisbottle and somebody, I'll swear,' exclaimed the radical in an energetic whisper, when they had listened for a few moments.

'Hush—pray let's hear what they say!' exclaimed Mrs. Tibbs, the gratification of whose curiosity was now paramount to every other consideration.

'Ah! if I could but believe you,' said a female voice coquettishly, 'I'd be bound to settle my missis for life.'

'What does she say?' inquired Mr. Evenson, who was not quite so well situated as his companion.

'She says she'll settle her missis's life,' replied Mrs. Tibbs. 'The wretch! they're plotting murder.'

'I know you want money,' continued the voice, which belonged to Agnes; 'and if you'd secure me the five hundred pound, I warrant she should take fire soon enough.'

'What's that?' inquired Evenson again. He could just hear enough to want to hear more.

'I think she says she'll set the house on fire,' replied the affrighted Mrs. Tibbs. 'But thank God I'm insured in the Phoenix!'

'The moment I have secured your mistress, my dear,' said a man's voice in a strong Irish brogue, 'you may depend on having the money.'

'Bless my soul, it's Mr. O'Bleary!' exclaimed Mrs. Tibbs, in a parenthesis.

'The villain!' said the indignant Mr. Evenson.

'The first thing to be done,' continued the Hibernian, 'is to poison Mr. Gobler's mind.'

'Oh, certainly,' returned Agnes.

'What's that?' inquired Evenson again, in an agony of curiosity and a whisper.

'He says she's to mind and poison Mr. Gobler,' replied Mrs. Tibbs, aghast at this sacrifice of human life.

'And in regard of Mrs. Tibbs,' continued O'Bleary.—Mrs. Tibbs shuddered.

'Hush!' exclaimed Agnes, in a tone of the greatest alarm, just as Mrs. Tibbs was on the extreme verge of a fainting fit. 'Hush!'

'Hush!' exclaimed Evenson, at the same moment to Mrs. Tibbs.

'There's somebody coming up-stairs,' said Agnes to O'Bleary.

'There's somebody coming down-stairs,' whispered Evenson to Mrs. Tibbs.

'Go into the parlour, sir,' said Agnes to her companion. 'You will get there, before whoever it is, gets to the top of the kitchen stairs.'

'The drawing-room, Mrs. Tibbs!' whispered the astonished Evenson to his equally astonished companion; and for the drawing-room they both made, plainly hearing the rustling of two persons, one coming down-stairs, and one coming up.

'What can it be?' exclaimed Mrs. Tibbs. 'It's like a dream. I wouldn't be found in this situation for the world!'

'Nor I,' returned Evenson, who could never bear a joke at his own expense. 'Hush! here they are at the door.'

'What fun!' whispered one of the new-comers.—It was Wisbottle.

'Glorious!' replied his companion, in an equally low tone.—This was Alfred Tomkins. 'Who would have thought it?'

'I told you so,' said Wisbottle, in a most knowing whisper. 'Lord bless you, he has paid her most extraordinary attention for the last two months. I saw 'em when I was sitting at the piano to-night.'

'Well, do you know I didn't notice it?' interrupted Tomkins.

'Not notice it!' continued Wisbottle. 'Bless you; I saw him whispering to her, and she crying; and then I'll swear I heard him say something about to-night when we were all in bed.'

'They're talking of us!' exclaimed the agonised Mrs. Tibbs, as the painful suspicion, and a sense of their situation, flashed upon her mind.

'I know it—I know it,' replied Evenson, with a melancholy consciousness that there was no mode of escape.

'What's to be done? we cannot both stop here!' ejaculated Mrs. Tibbs, in a state of partial derangement.

'I'll get up the chimney,' replied Evenson, who really meant what he said.

'You can't,' said Mrs. Tibbs, in despair. 'You can't—it's a register stove.'

'Hush!' repeated John Evenson.

'Hush—hush!' cried somebody down-stairs.

'What a d-d hushing!' said Alfred Tomkins, who began to get rather bewildered.

'There they are!' exclaimed the sapient Wisbottle, as a rustling noise was heard in the store-room.

'Hark!' whispered both the young men.

'Hark!' repeated Mrs. Tibbs and Evenson.

'Let me alone, sir,' said a female voice in the store-room.

'Oh, Hagnes!' cried another voice, which clearly belonged to Tibbs, for nobody else ever owned one like it, 'Oh, Hagnes—lovely creature!'

'Be quiet, sir!' (A bounce.)

'Hag—'

'Be quiet, sir—I am ashamed of you. Think of your

wife, Mr. Tibbs. Be quiet, sir!'

'My wife!' exclaimed the valorous Tibbs, who was clearly under the influence of gin-and-water, and a misplaced attachment; 'I ate her! Oh, Hagnes! when I was in the volunteer corps, in eighteen hundred and—'

'I declare I'll scream. Be quiet, sir, will you?' (Another bounce and a scuffle.)

'What's that?' exclaimed Tibbs, with a start.

'What's what?' said Agnes, stopping short.

'Why that!'

'Ah! you have done it nicely now, sir,' sobbed the frightened Agnes, as a tapping was heard at Mrs. Tibbs's bedroom door, which would have beaten any dozen woodpeckers hollow.

'Mrs. Tibbs! Mrs. Tibbs!' called out Mrs. Bloss. 'Mrs. Tibbs, pray get up.' (Here the imitation of a woodpecker was resumed with tenfold violence.)

'Oh, dear—dear!' exclaimed the wretched partner of the depraved Tibbs. 'She's knocking at my door. We must be discovered! What will they think?'

'Mrs. Tibbs! Mrs. Tibbs!' screamed the woodpecker again.

'What's the matter!' shouted Gobler, bursting out of the back drawing-room, like the dragon at Astley's.

'Oh, Mr. Gobler!' cried Mrs. Bloss, with a proper approximation to hysterics; 'I think the house is on fire, or else there's thieves in it. I have heard the most dreadful noises!'

'The devil you have!' shouted Gobler again, bouncing back into his den, in happy imitation of the aforesaid dragon, and returning immediately with a lighted candle. 'Why, what's this? Wisbottle! Tomkins! O'Bleary! Agnes! What the deuce! all up and dressed?'

'Astonishing!' said Mrs. Bloss, who had run downstairs, and taken Mr. Gobler's arm.

'Call Mrs. Tibbs directly, somebody,' said Gobler, turning into the front drawing-room.—'What! Mrs. Tibbs and Mr. Evenson!!'

'Mrs. Tibbs and Mr. Evenson!' repeated everybody, as that unhappy pair were discovered: Mrs. Tibbs seated in an arm-chair by the fireplace, and Mr. Evenson standing by her side,

We must leave the scene that ensued to the reader's imagination. We could tell, how Mrs. Tibbs forthwith fainted away, and how it required the united strength of Mr. Wisbottle and Mr. Alfred Tomkins to hold her in her chair; how Mr. Evenson explained, and how his explanation was evidently disbelieved; how Agnes repelled the accusations of Mrs. Tibbs by proving that she was negotiating with Mr. O'Bleary to influence her mistress's affections in his behalf; and how Mr. Gobler threw a damp counterpane on the hopes of Mr. O'Bleary by avowing that he (Gobler) had already proposed to, and been accepted by, Mrs. Bloss; how Agnes was discharged from that lady's service; how Mr. O'Bleary discharged himself from Mrs. Tibbs's house, without going through the form of previously discharging his bill; and how that disappointed young gentleman rails against England and the English, and vows there is no virtue or fine feeling extant, 'except in Ireland.' We repeat that we could tell all this, but we love to exercise our self-denial, and we therefore prefer leaving it to be imagined.

The lady whom we have hitherto described as Mrs. Bloss, is no more. Mrs. Gobler exists: Mrs. Bloss has left us for ever. In a secluded retreat in Newington Butts, far, far removed from the noisy strife of that great boarding-house, the world, the enviable Gobler and his pleasing wife revel in retirement: happy in their complaints, their table, and their medicine, wafted through life by the grateful prayers of all the purveyors of animal food within three miles round.

We would willingly stop here, but we have a painful duty imposed upon us, which we must discharge. Mr. and Mrs. Tibbs have separated by mutual consent, Mrs. Tibbs receiving one moiety of 43l. 15s. 10d., which we before stated to be the amount of her husband's annual income, and Mr. Tibbs the other. He is spending the evening of his days in retirement; and he is spending also, annually, that small but honourable independence. He resides among the original settlers at Walworth; and it has been stated, on unquestionable authority, that the conclusion of the volunteer story has been heard in a small tavern in that respectable neighbourhood.

The unfortunate Mrs. Tibbs has determined to dispose of the whole of her furniture by public auction, and to retire from a residence in which she has suffered so much. Mr. Robins has been applied to, to conduct the sale, and the transcendent abilities of the literary gentlemen connected with his establishment are now devoted to the task of drawing up the preliminary advertisement. It is to contain, among a variety of brilliant matter, seventy-eight words in large capitals, and six original quotations in inverted commas.

THE END

<u>RISE OF DOUAI</u>

RISE OF DOUAI

TWITTER : @RISEOFDOUAI

© 2013, PUBLISHED BY RISE OF DOUAI PUBLISHING, OTHER PUBLICATIONS:

- AN IDIOT'S GUIDE TO: BEE HUNTING BY JOHN LOCKARD, EDITED BY ARSALAN AHMED (2012)(PAPERBACK) ISBN-10: 1478383550

- THE RISE OF DOUAI BY ARSALAN AHMED (2012)(PAPERBACK) ISBN-10: 1479267783

- THE RICHEST MAN IN BABYLON BY GEORGE S. CLASON (2012) (PAPERBACK) ISBN-10: 1479377341

- THINK AND GROW RICH BY NAPOLEON HILL (2012) (PAPERBACK) ISBN-10: 1480061638

- AS A MAN THINKETH BY MR JAMES ALLEN (2012) (PAPERBACK) ISBN-10: 1480088161
- HOW TO ANALYZE PEOPLE ON

SIGHT BY ELSIE BENEDICT
(PAPERBACK) ISBN-10: 1480081272
- THE ART OF WAR BY MR SUN TZU (PAPERBACK) ISBN-10: 1480082007
- MACBETH BY MR WILLIAM SHAKESPEARE (PAPERBACK) ISBN-10: 1480060682
- A CHRISTMAS CAROL BY MR CHARLES DICKENS ISBN-10: 1481194755
- CREATING CAPITAL: MONEY-MAKING AS AN AIM IN BUSINESS BY MR FREDRICK L LIPMAN ISBN-10: 1481158996
- GETTING GOLD: A PRACTICAL TREATISE FOR PROSPECTORS, MINERS, AND STUDENTS BY MR JOSEPH COLIN FRANCIS JOHNSON ISBN-10: 1481090984
- THE INTERPRETATION OF DREAMS BY MR SIGMUND FREUD ISBN-10: 1481134558
- THE COMMUNIST MANIFESTO BY MR KARL MARX AND MR FRIDRICK ENGLES ISBN-10:

1480112445
- THE PRINCE BY MR NICCOLO MACHIAVELLI ISBN-10: 1480119601
- THE WAY TO WEALTH BY MR BENJAMIN FRANKLIN ISBN-10: 1480099651
- THE ART OF MONEY GETTING - OR GOLDEN RULES FOR MAKING MONEY (SUCCESS PRINCIPLES) BY MR PHINEAS TAYLOR BARNUM ISBN-10: 1480138622

Twitter : **@RiseofDouai**

Printed in Poland
by Amazon Fulfillment
Poland Sp. z o.o., Wrocław